For Esmé
B.F.

"Quack!" Said the Billy-Goat
Text copyright © 1970 by Charles Causley
Illustrations copyright © 1986 by Barbara Firth
Published in England by Walker Books Ltd., London.
Printed in Italy. All rights reserved.
10 9 8 7 6 5 4 3 2 1
First American Edition

Library of Congress Cataloging in Publication Data
Causley, Charles,
    "Quack!" said the billy-goat.

    Summary: Something is wrong in the barnyard when
goats quack and hens oink. What could the problem be?
    [1. Domestic animals—Fiction. 2. Humorous stories.
3. Stories in rhyme] I. Firth, Barbara, ill. II. Title.
PZ8.3.C3134Qac 1986b   [E]   85-23856
ISBN 0-397-32192-9 (lib. bdg.)

"QUACK!"
Said the Billy-Goat

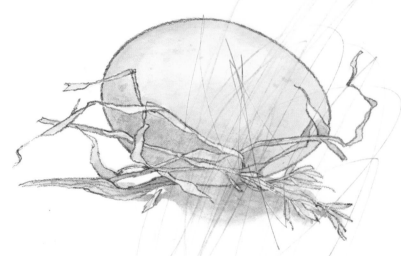

BY

Charles Causley

PICTURES BY

Barbara Firth

J. B. Lippincott   New York

"Quack!" said the billy-goat.

"Oink!" said the hen.

"Meow!" said the little chick
running in the pen.

"Gobble-gobble!" said the dog.

"Cluck!" said the sow.

"Whoo! Whoo!" the donkey said.

"Baa!" said the cow.

"Hee-haw!" the turkey cried.

The duck began to moo.

All at once the sheep called,

"Cock-a-doodle-doo!"

The owl coughed and
cleared his throat
and he began to bleat.
"Bow-wow!" the rooster said
swimming in the heat.

"Cheep–cheep!" said the cat
as she began to fly.

"Farmer Brown has laid an egg —
that's the reason why."